The KNIGHT and the DRAGON

STORY AND PICTURES BY
TOMIE dePAOLA

A TRUMPET CLUB SPECIAL EDITION

ISBN 0-590-98036-X

Copyright © 1980 by Tomie de Paola.
All rights reserved.
Published by Scholastic Inc., 555 Broadway, New York, NY 10012,
by arrangement with G. P. Putnam's Sons,
a division of The Putnam & Grosset Group.
TRUMPET and the TRUMPET logo are registered trademarks
of Scholastic Inc.

12 11 10 9 8 7 6 5 4 3 2   9/9 0 1/0

Printed in the U.S.A.

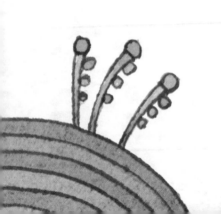

Once upon a time, there was a knight in a castle who had never fought a dragon.

And in a cave not too far away was a dragon who had never fought a knight.

One day the knight went to the castle library and took out
all of the books he could find on dragon fighting.

Meanwhile, back at the cave, the dragon had rummaged through all the things from his ancestors and found some books on knight fighting.

The knight began to build some armor.

The dragon practiced swishing his tail.

Meanwhile, back at the castle...

Meanwhile, back at the cave...

Finally, the knight and the dragon were both ready.
They sent each other a letter and set a time for...

the fight.